Moonlight and Mermaids

Collect all the Charmseekers -

The Queen's Bracelet
The Silver Pool
The Dragon's Revenge
A Tale of Two Sisters
The Fragile Force
The Stolen Goblet
The Magic Crystals
Secret Treasure
Star Island
Moonlight and Mermaids

From 2012
The Mirror of Deception
Zorgan and the Gorsemen
The Last Portal

www.charmseekers.co.uk

CHARMSEEKERS: BOOK TEN

Moonlight and Mermaids

Georgie Adams

Illustrated by Gwen Millard

Orion
Children's Books

First published in Great Britain in 2009
by Orion Children's Books
Reissued 2011 by Orion Children's Books
a division of the Orion Publishing Group Ltd
Orion House
5 Upper St Martin's Lane
London WC2H 9EA
An Hachette UK Company

1 3 5 7 9 8 6 4 2

The Orion Publishing Group's policy is to use papers that are natural,
renewable and recyclable products and made from wood grown in sustainable
forests. The logging and manufacturing processes are expected to conform
to the environmental regulations of the country of origin.

A catalogue record for this book is available from the British Library.

ISBN 978 1 4440 0298 0

Printed and bound in the UK by CPI Group (UK), Croydon, CR0 4YY

www.orionbooks.co.uk
www.charmseekers.co.uk

In fond memory of Selina Young –
free spirit, sadly missed

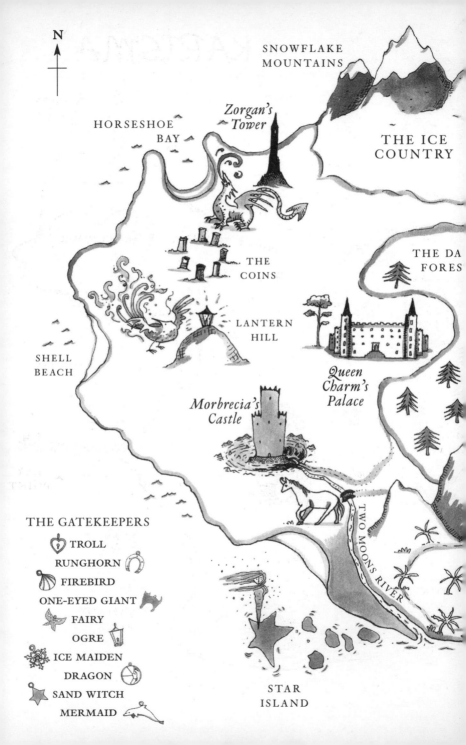

N

SNOWFLAKE
MOUNTAINS

*Zorgan's
Tower*

HORSESHOE
BAY

THE ICE
COUNTRY

THE DA
FORES

THE
COINS

LANTERN
HILL

SHELL
BEACH

*Queen
Charm's
Palace*

*Morbrecia's
Castle*

THE GATEKEEPERS

TWO MOONS RIVER

TROLL

RUNGHORN

FIREBIRD

ONE-EYED GIANT

FAIRY

OGRE

ICE MAIDEN

DRAGON

SAND WITCH

MERMAID

STAR
ISLAND

The Thirteen Charms of Karisma

When Charm became queen of Karisma, the wise and beautiful Silversmith made her a precious gift. It was a bracelet. On it were fastened thirteen silver amulets, which the Silversmith called 'charms', in honour of the new queen.

It was part of Karisma law. Whenever there was a new ruler the Silversmith made a special gift, to help them care for the world they had inherited. And this time it was a bracelet. She told Queen Charm it was magical because the charms held the power to control the forces of nature and keep everything in balance. She must take the greatest care of them. As long as she, and she alone, had possession of the charms all would be well.

And so it was, until the bracelet was stolen by a spider, and fell into the hands of Zorgan, the magician. Then there was chaos!

One

A wall of water rose from the sea and came thundering towards Sesame. She clung tight to her pony's mane as they galloped along the shore – Silver's flying hooves kicking up the sand. Chasing them was Princess Morbrecia astride a giant crab! The crab scuttled sideways at an alarming speed, gaining on Sesame fast. When Sesame dared to look back, she saw Morbrecia's hair, a tangled mass of seaweed, streaming behind her in the wind. Suddenly Morbrecia's skinny arm shot out to snatch Sesame's locket and . . .

Sesame woke.

"NO!" she screamed. "No! Go away!"

Nic Brown came bursting into her room to see what was the matter. He looked puzzled as his daughter sat up in bed, shaking her head.

"What's up, Ses?" he asked. "I heard you shouting. Thought you'd been attacked by aliens!"

4

"Er, no, Dad," said Sesame. She felt silly. "I had a crazy dream, that's all. I was riding Silver and there was this massive wave and . . . oh, it doesn't matter—"

Her voice trailed off. How could she explain about Morbrecia and the crab and everything she'd seen on Star Island* a while ago? She hadn't told him, or her gran, Lossy, about *any* of her adventures in magical Karisma and her quest to find the thirteen silver charms. No one knew, except her special friends Maddy, Gemma and Liz, who'd been there too. They were all Charmseekers and their club was top secret!

Sesame hated keeping secrets from her dad, but she knew he'd never believe her. Who would?! He'd think she was bonkers, or just making it up. One day she *would* try to explain everything – but not yet.

Nic smiled at her reassuringly.

"You were riding Silver yesterday, weren't you? And today we're going to Water Wonderland, with a super wave machine and slides. I heard you chatting about it, before you went to bed. I reckon it all got muddled up in your dream."

* *
✶ Do you remember what happened there? You can read about Sesame's adventure in Book Nine: *Star Island*

Sesame nodded. It was true she *had* been looking forward to going to Water Wonderland for ages.

"I can't wait to go, Dad," she said.

While Nic was making breakfast, Sesame quickly washed, dressed and bundled her swimming things into a kit bag. She was longing to wear the fab new stripy swimsuit her gran had bought her.

Sesame was halfway through the door, when she saw her necklace on the bedside table — a silver chain and locket, with tiny pictures of her parents inside — the one Morbrecia had tried to snatch (and *almost* got away with) the last time Sesame was in Karisma. That was how the clasp came to be broken but, since then, it had been repaired. She went back for her locket, put it on and ran downstairs. She found her dad in the kitchen, on the phone.

"Uh-huh . . . right . . . sorry to hear that, Mrs Green. Yes, I'll tell Sesame.

Hope Gemma will be okay. Thanks for letting me know. Bye."

"What's happened?" asked Sesame, dumping her kit bag on the floor.

"Gemma can't come today," said Nic, replacing the handset. "She's sprained her ankle playing football with her brother."

"Oh no!" wailed Sesame. "Poor Gemma."

Seconds later, her mobile jingled.

I SO WANTED 2 CUM 2DAY. MEGA MIZZ. ☹ HAVE FUN WITH MADDY + LIZ LUV GEMMA x

Sesame replied straightaway:

WE WILL MISS U LOADS. TELL U ABOUT WW L8R. HOPE UR BETTER SOON. ☺ LOL SESAME x

Lossy arrived after breakfast. She was going to help look after the girls. Nic had been booked to take photographs at the opening of the new leisure park; he hoped to get some good pictures of Sesame and her friends trying out the waterslides and other rides. Sesame had arranged to meet her best friend, Maddy Webb, and Liz Robinson there, at eleven o'clock sharp.

Liz was waiting for them, but there was no sign of Maddy. After several anxious minutes, Sesame looked at her watch.

"Eleven-ten," she said. "Why is Maddy *always* late?"

"Here she comes," said Lossy. She waved to Mrs Webb, who'd just dropped her daughter off in the car. Maddy ran up to them, full of apologies.

"Sorry, Mr Brown . . . forgot my towel . . . had to go back . . . Mum mad and—"

Sesame rolled her eyes and grinned at Maddy.

"That's okay, Maddy," said Nic. "Glad you could make it!"

Once inside, Lossy took the girls off to a changing room. The girls chatted excitedly, admiring each other's swimsuits. Maddy wore a spotty tankini top with sea-green shorts; Liz looked great in coral pink and Sesame's stripy swimsuit fitted perfectly.

Sesame was about to leave her watch and necklace in a locker, when she read a warning notice:

> **The management regrets it cannot accept responsibility for the loss or theft of personal property. Please keep valuables with you at all times!**

So she decided to keep them on.

Lossy and the girls met up again with Nic, at the Mermaid Café. He'd been enjoying a tropical fruit smoothie while he was waiting for them.

"Where would you like to start?" he asked. "The Rocky Creek raft ride looks fun."

"Yesssss!" chorused the girls at once.

"Too scary for me," said Lossy. "I'll settle for a Pineapple Surprise and wait for you here."

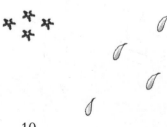

Sesame, Maddy and Liz shrieked with delight as they were buffeted about in a raft, crashing and splashing down a fast and furious creek, while Nic took action-packed pictures.

Next, they jumped over waves in the Dolphin Lagoon, and dashed through Thunder Valley Falls. Finally, they joined the queue waiting to go on The Crazy Octopus.

"For experienced swimmers only," Liz read from a safety sign. She added half-jokingly, "I'm glad I've got my life-saving certificate!"

They heard screams coming from one white-knuckle waterslide and Maddy felt her knees go wobbly.

"Mm," she said. "You might have to rescue me!"

"You'll be okay," said Sesame. "We'll race each other to the pool."

"I'll wait and see who wins," said Nic. "I should get some good pictures. Good luck!"

The girls climbed a flight of steps, then each sat at the entrance to a chute. From there the slides looked terrifying – long, twisty tubes, snaking to the pool far below.

Sesame suddenly felt her necklace tingle, sending a prickling sensation down her spine. She had the weirdest feeling something magical, something extraordinary, was about to happen. No time to think. Behind her was a queue of people waiting their turns on the slides. She looked at Maddy and Liz.

12

Two

The Silversmith wanders through the woods on Mount Fortuna. It is a beautiful moonlit night in the mede* of Carm, at the beginning of summer.

* *

⭐ **Mede** – month

She breathes deeply and enjoys the fresh smell of the pine forest; and as she walks, she thinks about recent events. News of Sesame has reached her in various ways: whispers, rumours, urchin and fairy gossip.

"I knew the moment Sesame was parted from her locket," she murmurs. "I felt the wrench of losing contact with my Seeker. It *mustn't* happen again. If only I could find a way to protect her from Zorgan, the magician—" She stops. Listens. She has heard the faintest flutter of wings. Is it a bird, or perhaps a moon moth?

It is neither. To the Silversmith's delight, she glimpses a fairy flitting through the trees – her green, gossamer gown, shimmering in the moonlight. When the fairy settles on the path in front of her, the Silversmith sees the delicate features of a girl.

She smiles sweetly at the Silversmith and greets her:

"Fairnight,* Metalcharmer. I am Quilla."

* *
Fairnight – a typical greeting, after moonrise

15

The Silversmith is amused to be called Metalcharmer, which she knows is the fairy name for a silversmith. Fairies believe silversmiths can charm metal, and have the greatest respect for their skills.

"Fairnight, Quilla," replies the Silversmith. "I'm pleased we meet at last."

"You fear for your Seeker from the Outworld,"* says Quilla. It is not a question.

"Yes," says the Silversmith. She is not surprised that Quilla knows what she has been thinking. "Sesame Brown is in grave danger. Zorgan is determined to put a curse on Sesame, to make her bring him the charms. For such powerful sorcery to work, he must hold something precious that belongs to her. He has been trying to steal her locket."

Quilla sighs.

"I'm afraid the magician will succeed," she says. "As you know I live backwards. I have seen the future. Zorgan *will* take possession of Sesame's locket. It is only a matter of time!"

Later, when the Silversmith returns to her workshop, her thoughts are in a whirl. She paces the floor, thinking. Thinking!

"Is there no way I can prevent Sesame losing her locket?" she says. "I know Sesame would never willingly give Zorgan the charms, but if she falls under his spell . . . oh, the consequences are too terrible to imagine! That balam* magician will empower Charm's bracelet with Dark Magic. Morbrecia will wear it and become queen, but it is Zorgan who will be in control. *He* will rule Karisma. No! I can't let this happen. There must be *something* I can do . . ."

Three

WHOOOOOOSH!

Sesame flew along the red chute — flat on her back, feet first. All the way down she had the strangest feeling she was floating on air, the wind whistling past her ears. Maddy was on the blue slide, Liz on the green. The girls were flipped this way and that as they whizzed around the twisty waterslides, until they shot into the pool —

It's like a bubble bath, thought Sesame, swimming underwater. But when she opened her eyes, she noticed something strange about the bubbles — they were going the wrong way. She knew bubbles in fizzy drinks travelled up, but these were definitely going down — and they were pulling her with them!

She looked around for Maddy and Liz; they seemed to be turning somersaults in slow motion and, when she tried calling them, no sound came out. Next thing she knew they were all tumbling, like clothes in a washing machine, faster and faster – down, down, down in a swirl of bubbles – on their way to Karisma!

POP! POP! POP!

The girls surfaced by a big rock in the sea, bathed in silvery moonlight. The water felt cold, so they quickly clambered out onto the rocky ledge. Which is when they noticed the mermaid.

"Wow!" exclaimed Maddy.

"A real mermaid!" said Liz, shaking drops of seawater off her glasses.

They stared at her in wonder. She was sitting in a magnificent oyster shell, her rainbow-coloured tail

swept elegantly to one side; around her neck she wore strings of fine pearls and entwined in her long, fair hair were the brightest red moon poppies. * She was playing a scallop-shell harp and singing:

Beneath two brightly shining moons,
Dolphins dance to mermaids' tunes.
While far below the foaming waves,
Merfolk stir, in coral caves.
Whispering tales about the sea,
Moonshine magic and mystery!

The mermaid saw the girls and waved.

"Fairnight, Charmseekers," she said. "Welcome back to Karisma. I'm Selena, Gatekeeper Ten. This is Mermaid Rock."

"Hi," said Sesame.

"I'm Maddy," said Maddy, "and this is Liz and—"

"Sesame Brown," said Selena. "Yes, we gatekeepers know all about you. Queen Charm told us you're looking for her missing charms." Selena paused. Sesame's necklace had caught her eye.

* *
* Moon poppy – a type of sea flower, found only in waters around Karisma

21

Mermaids love jewellery. "Ah, this is the locket I've heard so much about."

"Er, yes," said Sesame.

She looked slightly puzzled, so Selena explained:

"My friend Ramora the sand witch whispered a message in the waves. It arrived a while ago on the evening tide. It's a pretty locket. May I see inside?"

"Of course," said Sesame, opening it to show Selena the pictures of her parents. "My mum Poppy died in a car accident, when I was a baby."

22

It was Selena's turn to look puzzled.

"Car?"

Liz did her best to describe one.

"It has wheels and seats and doors and a motor and you . . . drive it around," she finished flatly. She could tell Selena hadn't a clue what she was talking about.

"Whatever it is," said Selena, "I'm very sorry to hear about your mother, Sesame."

"Thanks," said Sesame, firmly closing her locket with a *snap!* "When Mum died, my dad gave me her special jewellery box. It's where I'm keeping the charms." Then thinking Selena might get the wrong idea, she hastily added: "Of course, I'll be returning them to the queen when we've found them all!"

"Four are still missing," said Maddy.

"I think I can remember what they are," said Liz. "The moon, the lucky cloverleaf, the dolphin and the . . . key."

"Sesame Brown will track them down!" said Sesame.

"Well, I hope you find them soon," said the gatekeeper. "Ever since the queen's bracelet was stolen, I've noticed changes. The wind has been blowing the wrong way and the sea has got colder. All is not well for us merfolk."

23

"I think the sea is colder because the ice is melting in the Ice Country," explained Sesame. "You see, the charms help control the forces of nature. Things won't get better till they're all back together again. And I won't give up till I've found them! I wonder which one we'll find this time."

She glanced at the brightly shining moons. Perhaps they'd find the crescent moon. Selena knew what Sesame was thinking.

"Look below the waves," she advised. "You may find the *dolphin* there."

"Oh," said Sesame. "I love dolphins! They're SO playful. I saw this brill programme on TV once and—"

She broke off. Liz was looking worried.

"Um, how do we breathe underwater?" Liz asked Selena.

"Yeah," said Maddy. "Big problem."

"Follow the seahorse," said Selena. "He will help you."

"Thanks," said Sesame. "What time do we have to be back?"

"Sunrise," said Selena.

Sesame looked at her watch. The digital display had magically changed to Karisma time. It had happened before, and now the dial looked like this:

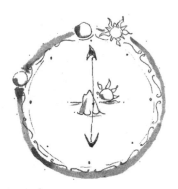

"I'm glad my watch is waterproof!" she said.
And they dived into the chilly sea.

The bandrall,* Vanda, had seen and heard everything. Selena saw her take off from Mermaid Rock, soar into the sky and fly north, towards Zorgan's Tower. She knew it was a bad sign. It sent a shiver down her tail.

* *
* **Bandrall** – rare flying mammal, native to Karisma

Four

From his Star Room, Zorgan searched the starry heavens, waiting for the return of Vanda. He'd sent her to spy out the land. While he waited, he marvelled at the moons.

"They are at their brightest and best at this time of year," he murmured. "A magical sight! No doubt the Moon Spirits are celebrating tonight . . ."

His thoughts were suddenly interrupted by the sound of leathery wings, beating at the window. It was Vanda. Zorgan let her in and she perched on a chair, while he fed her choice morsels of toad liver and worms.

"Anything to report?" he asked.

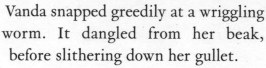

Vanda snapped greedily at a wriggling worm. It dangled from her beak, before slithering down her gullet.

"Mermaid Rock," she croaked. "Sesame Brown and two others. Seeking under the sea."

"Spallah!"* exclaimed Zorgan, delighted the Charmseekers were back. "Was Sesame wearing her locket?"

Vanda gobbled a titbit of toad, then replied:

"Pictures inside."

"What pictures?" snapped Zorgan.

"Parents," said Vanda. "Poppy."

"Ah!" said Zorgan. "Better than I thought. You have done well."

For a while the magician was deep in thought. He paced the floor of his Star Room, fiddling with a gold medallion. Before long, the corners of his lips curled into a cruel smile.

"I have an idea," he said.

* *

*Spallah — excellent. A triumphant expression

Zorgan summoned Nix and Dina to his library, where he kept his magnificent collection of spell books. The pixie girls were by his side in an instant, their sharp crystal eyes glinting in anticipation, eager to carry out their master's wishes.

"You will go to Mermaid Rock and find Sesame Brown," said Zorgan. "I'm giving you one last chance to bring me her locket. If you fail, I'll turn you into fishpaste!"

"Yes, Master!" they chorused, shuddering at the venom in his voice. It was true, their previous attempts to steal Sesame's locket *had* failed, but they were determined to succeed this time. If they didn't, they knew Zorgan would carry out his threat. Nix and Dina whirred their wings, in readiness to take off, but Zorgan held up his hand.

"Stop! I haven't finished. For this mission I'll be making a slight alteration to your appearance. A temporary disguise to fool Sesame and assist you in your task . . ."

The pixies were programmed to obey Zorgan without question. Nevertheless, they couldn't help wondering what he had in store for them.

Apprehensively, they watched as he opened his spell book (at a page he'd previously marked) and twitched his magic wand. Flashing lights and fizzing sparks flew from the wand as he pointed at each pixie and intoned:

"With steely wings and fishy tail,
A mermaid you shall be.
Make haste and dare not think to fail –
I must curse S–e–s–a–m–e!"

The spell worked straightaway and took the pixies by surprise. Their legs changed into scaly fish tails and they felt most peculiar. Besides, they couldn't stand up.

"Woooah!"

cried Nix, falling flat on her face.

"Whoops!"

shrieked Dina, wobbling about. She flipped and flapped her tail, trying to get her balance.

Zorgan wasn't amused. "Doofers!"* he yelled. "Flap your wings. You're *flying* mermaids! Get going and don't come back without the locket."

* *
✫ **Doofer** – idiot of the first order. Brainless

31

The Silversmith, meanwhile, has been thinking about her Seeker. She glances at the thirteen magic candles — four remain burning brightly for their charms yet to be found. She crosses her workshop to stand by the window. The silvery moons bathe her in pools of light as she recalls her chance meeting with Quilla.

"If Quilla is right, if Zorgan steals Sesame's locket I must thwart his plans. I *am* a metalcharmer. I made the magical charm bracelet. I have mystic powers over all things silver. . ."

She closes her eyes. Soon she is in a dreamlike state, and into her dreams drift the gentle Moon Spirits. They take the Silversmith by the hand and fly with her to Mermaid Rock, whispering the whereabouts of Sesame — and a magical charm, waiting to be found.

The Moon Spirits cast their shimmering beams below the waves. Now the Silversmith sees her Seeker, glimpses her silver locket . . . and, in her trance, she softly murmurs:

Gentle moonbeams shining bright.
Cast your magic spell tonight!"

In the blink of an eye, she is awake. The Moon
Spirits have gone, but memories of all she has seen
and heard in her dream remain.

"The Moon Spirits will help Sesame tonight," she
says. "I don't know how, but they will."

Five

Sesame, Maddy and Liz found the seahorse waiting for them.

"Follow me," he said. "I'll take you to the Mer Elder."

The pearly-pink seahorse with its tube-like nose, spiny body and curly tail led the girls down through freezing, green waters to the seabed. They passed a mother dolphin and her calf playing with a piece of seaweed, 'talking' to each other in clicks and whistles.

Sesame was amazed to discover she could understand their language.

"They're playing seaweed tag!" she told Maddy and Liz.

Maddy was just wondering how much longer she could hold her breath, when the seahorse stopped at a grotto. Moonbeams shone through crystal windows, so the girls could see everything clearly. As they looked around, their eyes opened wide in astonishment. The walls and roof were decorated with exquisite mosaics, made from thousands of tiny shells, pearls and precious stones – pictures of sea-dragons, mermaids, dolphins and whales; brightly-coloured coral and strange-looking fish.

In the middle of the grotto stood a white marble fountain, which was spouting bubbles. Some mermaids were having a game with one bubble, big as beach ball, flicking it about with their tails.

"I wish we had tails," said Liz. "It looks fun."

The others nodded.

"Bubbleball," said the seahorse. "It's a favourite game down here. It helps to keep them warm. If they didn't, their tails would turn blue with cold! Now come and meet the Mer Elder."

35

The Mer Elder was sitting on a clamshell; he wore
a gold ring in one ear and had spiky orange hair.

"I'm sure he can help you," said the seahorse.

"I hope so," said Maddy. "I'm gasping for some
air!"

"Welcome, Charmseekers," said the Mer Elder.
"If it's air you need, come with me."

36

He swam to the fountain and scooped up some bubbles.

"Long lasting air bubbles," said the Mer Elder. "Swallow these and you'll breath like fish." He blew the bubbles at them and said some magic words:

"GILL INFLATIMUS AORTA!"

After taking deep breaths, Sesame, Maddy and Liz felt much better.

By now the girls were surrounded by inquisitive merfolk. They'd heard about the famous Charmseekers and wanted to see what they looked like! One mermaid, who'd been playing bubbleball, came forward.

"I'm Meranda," she said.

"Hi," said Sesame, and she introduced the others.

"Pretty beads," said Maddy, admiring the glass necklace Meranda was wearing. "It's like the one I found on Star Island."

"I bought it from the urchins," said Meranda. "They make jewellery and ornaments from things they find on the beach. Urchin craft is very popular with mermaids."

"We know them," said Sesame. "It's great they're recycling their left-behindings."

"What *are* you talking about?" said Liz, who hadn't met the urchins.

"Tell you later," Sesame promised. "We *must* look for the charm."

"May I come?" asked Meranda. "I know the sea like the back of my tail."

The girls thought it was a great idea, so they showed her their Charmseekers secret hand sign.

"Now I'm a Charmseeker, too!" said Meranda proudly.

"Setfair,"* said the Mer Elder. "I hope you find all the charms soon, Sesame. If the sea gets much colder, we shall perish!"

"The charm could be anywhere," groaned Maddy.

Liz peered through her glasses at the vast expanse of sea.

"Mm," she agreed, "and we haven't much time to find it."

Sesame snatched a look at her watch.

"Yes," she said. "Karisma time is weird. The nights are shorter than ours. We must hurry." She turned to Meranda. "Where do you think we should start?"

"Dolphin Bay," suggested Meranda. "But if you haven't much time, the quickest way there is through a spooky kelp forest."

* *
*Setfair – goodbye and good luck

39

"Dolphin Bay sounds good," said Sesame. "Don't worry. If we keep together, we'll be okay."

So, with a flick of her tail, Meranda headed for Dolphin Bay. Sesame, Maddy and Liz were good swimmers; they could keep up with the mermaid quite easily. As they were rounding Key Point, Sesame was aware of sounds travelling through the water. She thought they sounded like the clicks and whistles she'd heard earlier – only these were different. The high-pitch tone of the signals told her something was wrong.

"Wait!" she cried. "That sounds like a dolphin. I think it's in trouble."

"I can't hear anything," said Maddy.

Liz strained her ears.

"Nope. Not a thing," she said.

"Sesame's right," said Meranda. "They're coming from the other side of the forest. Follow me!"

As soon as they entered the gloomy place, the Charmseekers felt a sense of foreboding. Meranda was right. The kelp forest *was* spooky! The giant seaweed towered tall as trees, their fronds waving in the murky water. Nothing grew here except kelp, and everywhere was eerily silent.

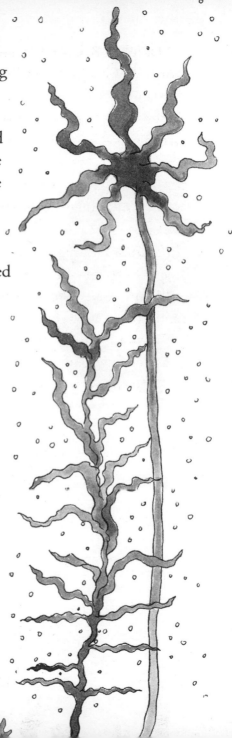

41

Sesame did her best to keep close to Meranda's tail, but the further they went, the gloomier it became, until *bump* – she swam headlong into a kelp stalk. It was slimy, and thick as a tree trunk.

Yuk!" she cried, pushing herself away with such force she accidentally turned a somersault. When Sesame tried to right herself, she realised she'd lost all sense of direction. Help! she thought. Which *is* the right way up? Worse still, she couldn't see Maddy, Liz or Meranda anywhere.

To her dismay, she was completely alone.

Six

Sesame shivered. It was icy cold and dark in the kelp forest. Even the moons couldn't shine their light here. Every so often the silence was broken by squeals of distress, which Sesame knew were coming from a dolphin. She took deep breaths to calm the panicky feeling welling up inside her tummy.

"Don't panic," she said. "Chill out! Think, Sesame. Think! If Sesame Brown can track charms down, finding Maddy, Liz and Meranda shouldn't be a problem. Right? Follow the signals and we *should* all meet up with the dolphins."

Sesame brushed aside trailing seaweed fronds which were grabbing at her hair, and began swimming towards the squeals. It wasn't long before she noticed two shadowy shapes moving below, and then her imagination ran wild. Oh, no! she thought. Girl-eating sharks! Her heart was pounding. She'd never felt so frightened. She was sure she'd be eaten alive. Suddenly Sesame came to a clearing, where moonbeams reached even these dark waters. Now she was relieved to see the shapes weren't sharks, they were mermaids!

Sesame's locket had started to tingle and goose pimples were running up and down her spine. Was it a good sign or a warning, she wondered, turning to face the oncoming mermaids. Perhaps Meranda had sent her friends to help. Yes, that was it!

But as the mermaids closed in, Sesame's locket tingled again and again and, just in time, she saw the glint of a steely wing in the shadowy moonlight . . .

She gasped in horror.

"You're not mermaids," she said. "You're Nix and Dina in disguise!"

"And *you're* in trouble!" said Nix gleefully.

44

"Give me your locket NOW," said Dina. "Or else."

The menacing pixie lunged at Sesame. She was quick, but Sesame was quicker. She jinxed behind a rock then, dodging both pixies, darted between the kelp like a fish.

By now, Sesame's eyesight had adjusted to the gloomy light and she swam scarily fast through the forest. Nix and Dina, finding it difficult to control their tails, kept getting tangled in seaweed! Although Sesame wasn't aware of it, she did have another advantage over the pixies; the dolphin had picked up Sesame's sound vibrations through the water, and was guiding her with *clicks* to Dolphin Bay. Nix and Dina heard them too, but they didn't know what they meant. Soon Sesame had left Nix and Dina behind — but they were determined to catch her up.

Through the Scary Kelp Forest

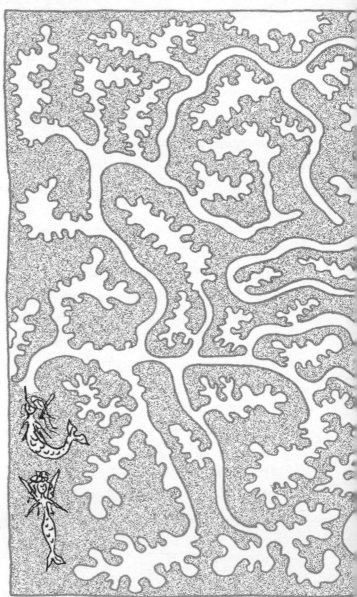

The pixies must catch Sesame and steal her locket. Can you see the path Nix and Dina must take to find her?

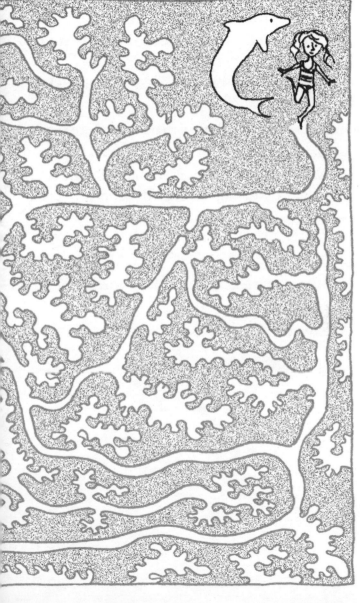

Sesame found the dolphin stranded on the seabed, tangled in fishing net. Nearby her calf was swimming in circles, whistling in distress.

"Oh, you poor thing!" cried Sesame, reaching through the net to stroke the dolphin's nose. "You must be exhausted. And you've injured your flippers."

Her thoughts raced. What could she do? She talked to herself, trying to think.

"Dolphins need air, I know that. But there's no way I can take her to the surface to breathe. Not on my own. Which reminds me, where *are* Maddy, Liz and Meranda? I SO hoped they'd be here. The dolphin must have air or she'll die!"

She looked around hoping, by some miracle, to see the others. But there was no sign of them – or, for that matter, of Nix and Dina.

"Phew!" she said. "At least I don't have to worry about the pixies!"

As she spoke, bubbles came popping out of her mouth – and *that* gave Sesame an idea . . .

"Magic bubbles!" she cried. "I'll give some of mine to the dolphin."

Sesame located the blowhole at the top of the dolphin's head, then she gently blew bubbles inside. To her delight it worked. The mother was out of immediate danger, and her calf flipped a somersault for joy. But she was still caught in the net.

"I'll soon have you out of there," Sesame promised.

However, untangling the net proved more difficult than Sesame imagined; it was tightly wound round her tail and flippers. While Sesame was struggling with it, she got her foot caught and then her arm got stuck. Twisting and kicking, she struggled to free herself, but it was no good.

She was snared
too! And just when she
thought things couldn't get
any worse — they suddenly did.
Nix and Dina finally caught up with her.

"Got you!" shrieked Nix, her eyes glinting with malicious pleasure. Her victim was wrapped like a parcel.

"Just where we want you," added Dina. "You don't stand a chance, Sesame Brown!" She made a grab for Sesame's locket.

"NO!" screamed Sesame. "Go away!"

Echoes of her nightmare rang in her head. Only this time her dad wasn't there to comfort her. This was for real! Sesame gripped Dina's wrist with her free hand. The pixie was pulling at her locket and Sesame could feel the chain cutting into her neck.

Now Nix was at her throat —
tugging, tugging, tugging at the
locket, until *SNAP!* The clasp broke.

"GOT IT!" cried Nix triumphantly,
holding Sesame's locket aloft.

"Our master shall have it at last!" said
Dina.

"NO!" wailed Sesame. "Give it back!
PLEASE!"

And none of them saw the monstrous octopus
swiftly heading their way . . .

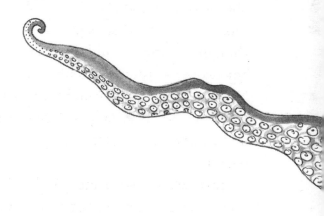

Seven

In another part of the forest, Maddy, Liz and Meranda had been searching for Sesame. For a while Meranda had followed the dolphin's signals but when they'd stopped, she'd lost her way.

"I'm sorry," she said. "It all looks strange."

"Never mind," said Liz. "I'm sure we'll find Sesame soon."

"If Ses doesn't find us first," said Maddy, trying to sound cheerful.

At last, they found a way out of the horrid forest and into Dolphin Bay. Bright moonbeams filtered through blue-green waters and shed their light on a coral reef. As they swam over it, Maddy and Liz saw shoals of strange-looking fish; and, clinging to the reef were purple sponges, pink anemones and delicate white sea-fans.

"Wow!" exclaimed Maddy. "It's like a tropical garden."

Liz noticed a clump of gorgeous bright red flowers.

"What are those?" she asked Meranda.

"Moon poppies," said the mermaid. "They only open their petals in the moonlight."

When Maddy looked again she saw something small, something *silver*, caught in the petals and glistening in the moonlight. She gasped.

"It's the dolphin charm!"

The others peered at it too.

"Oh!" sighed Meranda. "It's beautiful!"

"I *wish* Sesame was here," said Liz.

Maddy was reaching for the charm, when Meranda shouted a warning.

"Look out! Puffcap!"*

An enormous jellyfish topped with a blobby poison cap was hovering overhead, waving its tentacles. The girls backed away terrified.

"It looks like an alien!" said Liz.

"Puffcaps are very dangerous," said Meranda. "Moon poppies are their favourite food. They'll sting anything that gets in their way!"

Maddy glanced first at the charm then at the jellyfish, which was about to land on the poppy.

* *
*Puffcap – a large jellyfish, so called because its poison sack looks like a cap

"That puff-thing's going to eat it!" cried Maddy. "We can't risk losing the charm."

"R-i-g-h-t," said Liz, dodging a deadly tentacle. She'd been stung by a jellyfish once, and remembered how much it had hurt.

Thoughts whirled inside Maddy's head. What would Sesame do? I bet she wouldn't give up. Well, I'm a Charmseeker too! I've made up my mind . . .

"I'm going for the charm," she announced fearlessly.

"*Please* be careful, Maddy," Meranda pleaded. "Puffcaps can kill!"

Liz could tell Maddy was determined to rescue the charm, and tried to reassure her.

"You'll be okay," she said. "I've done my life-savers badge. I know how to rescue a casualty—"

"Er, yeah, thanks, Liz," Maddy cut in. "Let's hope I won't need your life-saving skills!"

They gave each other their secret hand sign for luck, then Maddy took a deep breath.

"Here goes!"

Everything happened quickly. As Maddy plucked the charm from the poppy, the puffcap shot out a stinging tentacle, whipping it around her wrist.

"Aaaaaaaargh!"

shrieked Maddy, dropping the charm.

It felt as if she'd being stung by a million wasps at once! Her head was spinning. She saw stars. She felt dizzy . . . then she couldn't remember a thing.

In a daze, Meranda watched the dolphin charm spiral slowly down, until it disappeared through a crack in the rock. Liz's eyes were fixed on Maddy, hanging in the water, limp and lifeless.

"I'm coming," she yelled. She took Maddy firmly by one arm and supported her chin, then with Meranda close behind, she towed her to the surface.

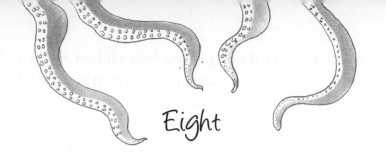

Eight

Meanwhile Sesame had been experiencing some hair-raising events of her own.

Trapped in the net with the dolphin, she could only stare wide-eyed at the giant octopus. Nix and Dina, who had their backs to the monster, mistook Sesame's petrified look for shock – they thought she was upset at losing her locket. But they soon realised their mistake. Swiftly, stealthily, the octopus came from behind and squirted them with smelly black ink! The pixies got the surprise of their lives.

"UGH!"

spluttered Nix, choking on the foul-tasting fluid.

"YUK!"

yelled Dina, swallowing a mouthful of ink.

57

In the confusion, Nix let go of the locket. Sesame saw it falling through the water. She pushed her free arm through the net, reaching, stretching as far as she could, in a desperate attempt to catch hold of it. For one exhilarating moment, she felt the chain brush the tips of her fingers – then it floated away.

As the inky water cleared, the pixies' laser-sharp eyes spotted the falling locket. Tears of frustration ran down Sesame's cheeks as she watched Nix and Dina dive for it. But the octopus was ready for them. His writhing tentacle seized Dina by her hair and flung her aside; he coiled another round Nix's tail and shook her like a rag doll.

"Ouch, ow, ow!" yelled Dina.

"Help! Stop!" cried Nix.

Suddenly, despite everything, Sesame giggled and whispered to the dolphins:

"I think the octopus is on our side!"

Nevertheless, the ruthless pixies hadn't forgotten their master's fish paste threat. Wrenching herself free, Dina snatched up the locket; then with a swish of their tails, the pixies swam off as fast as they could go.

Sesame was filled with dismay all over again – nothing could stop Zorgan casting his spell now!

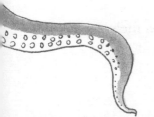

58

Sesame was right about the octopus. He *was* friendly!

"I came straightaway when I heard the distress calls," he told her. "When I saw those pixies I tried to help you, too. The merfolk said you were a Charmseeker!"

"You were brill," said Sesame.

The octopus helped Sesame from the net, then together they released the dolphin. They thanked the octopus for his help and he went home to his cave.

Sesame looked at her watch. Time was whizzing by! "It's *ages* since I saw Maddy, Liz and Meranda," she told the dolphins. "I wonder what's happened to them?"

Just then the dolphins picked up mermaid signals through the waves and Sesame knew something must be wrong.

"What's up?" she asked.

Your friends are in trouble. Come with me!

Nine

The Silversmith knew the instant Nix wrenched Sesame's locket away. A pain stabbed her chest and she saw a shadow fall across the moons.

"Hushish!"* So, Zorgan's wretched pixies have succeeded."

In her mind's eye she sees Sesame's locket, and again she implores the Moon Spirits:

> Gentle moonbeams shining bright
> Cast your magic spell tonight!"

Far from the clutches of the octopus, Nix and Dina leaped from the sea like flying fish. They landed *splat! smack!* on the peak of Mermaid Rock – where their tails fell off! Instantly, they were transformed into themselves.

* *
* Hushish – a word used to express dismay

"Good," said Nix, stretching her legs. "I hated that slimy fishtail!"

"Me, too," said Dina. "Now we can return to our master."

Before they took off, Dina couldn't resist holding Sesame's locket up to look at it. Her eyes sparkled with delight as she recalled the look of pain on Sesame's face. The locket shone in the moonlight . . .

Suddenly a moonbeam struck it like a bolt of lightning! Dina shielded herself from the blow; the locket sprang open – and out fell the picture of Poppy. Nix and Dina watched the tiny picture flutter away on a breeze.

"Leave it," said Nix. "We've got the locket. That's all that matters. Let's go!"

And with a whir of steely wings, the pixies flew off to Zorgan's Tower.

Selena the Gatekeeper was anxiously keeping watch for the Charmseekers' return.

"It will be sunrise soon," she said. "How strange! Tonight the moons are shining more brightly than ever."

As she spoke, a bright light struck Mermaid Rock. Selena saw a fragment of paper come spinning like a leaf – twisting and twirling, until it landed by her tail. The mermaid picked it up and gave a little gasp of surprise.

"This belongs to Sesame," she said, recognising the picture from Sesame's locket. "What can have happened?"

About this time, Sesame was being reunited with her friends. The dolphin mother and her calf had taken Sesame to Maddy, Liz and Meranda.

"Thank you," Meranda whispered to the dolphins.

Sesame was shocked when she saw Maddy – her best friend looked weak and pale. She listened while Liz described what happened. When she'd finished Meranda quickly added:

"Maddy was very lucky to survive the puffcap sting. They're deadly dangerous!"

"Oh, Maddy," said Sesame. "You were SO brave!"

"I feel a bit funny," said Maddy. "But, Ses, the dolphin charm! I dropped it—"

Her voice trailed away and she looked as if she was going to faint again. The dolphins gently held her with their flippers.

"I saw where the charm fell," said Meranda. "I'll take you there, Sesame."

Sesame looked at her watch. The sun was beginning to creep over the horizon.

"Great!" she said. "I reckon we've got about ten minutes left before sunrise. Come on. There's no time to lose!"

"I'll stay with Maddy," said Liz. "Good luck!"

Sesame dived with Meranda and followed the mermaid down to the coral reef. Moonbeams lit their way, which slightly puzzled Sesame, because it was nearly morning.

Soon they passed the patch of moon poppies Meranda and the girls had seen earlier. The mermaid looked cautiously around for the puffcap, but thankfully it was nowhere in sight. Eventually, they came to the place where the charm had disappeared.

"It went in there," said Meranda, pointing to a yawning crack in a rock.

Sesame peered in. She couldn't see a thing, until a shaft of moonlight caught a speck of silver. It twinkled like the brightest star in a black, velvet sky. Sesame's tummy flipped with excitement as she reached in . . . Her fingers closed around something small and smooth, and slowly she eased it out. It *was* the little dolphin charm! Even at this depth, the charm seemed to sparkle with a magical light of its own.

"Oh, it's fabulous," said Sesame, holding it so Meranda could see.

"It looks like a *real* dolphin," said Meranda.

Sesame clasped it in her hand, afraid she might lose it. For a split-second she thought of her locket slipping away, and she held the charm more tightly still. Can't worry about that now, thought Sesame. We must get back to the gate!

The dolphins took the Charmseekers for the ride of their lives – skimming, jumping, leaping over the foaming waves – all the way to Mermaid Rock!

Selena was at the gate.

"Hurry!" she urged the girls. "It's almost sunrise. Sesame, I have something for you." She held up a small mermaid purse. "It contains something precious."

"Thank you," said Sesame, briefly wondering what it could be. "Is there room for this, too?" She opened her palm to show Selena the dolphin charm. She thought the little purse would be the perfect place to put it.

"Of course," said Selena, opening the purse for Sesame to drop it in. "I'm delighted you found it. Well done, Charmseekers. Setfair!"

When Sesame, Maddy and Liz turned to go, there were loud cheers from Meranda, the Mer Elder and all the merfolk. A little way out to sea, the dolphins leaped for joy. The Mer Elder blew a stream of rainbow-coloured bubbles, then an enormous wave swept them off Mermaid Rock and they were plunged into a sea of sparkling, bubbling foam.

Down they went with the bubbles, past the little seahorse and the octopus, faster and faster, until –

Whooooosh! — they splashed into The Crazy Octopus pool, at Water Wonderland.

"Terrific!" said Nic. "Great action pic. You all arrived together!"

Sesame, Maddy and Liz scrambled out of the pool in a daze. The waterslides had been amazing, but nothing compared to their adventures in Karisma! And Sesame and Liz were still concerned about Maddy's jellyfish sting.

"Are you okay?" whispered Liz.

"I feel fine," said Maddy. "I think those bubbles did the trick!"

"Come on," said Nic. "Let's find Lossy. She's waiting for us at the Mermaid Café."

"Where's your locket, Sesame?" asked Lossy, as soon as they met up.

Maddy shot Sesame a look of startled surprise. It was the first time she'd noticed it was missing.

"Er, I must have lost it—" began Sesame.

"Oh, what a shame," exclaimed Lossy. "I expect you dropped it on one of the rides. Perhaps someone will find it and hand it in. You never know your luck."

✳ ✳ ✳

Later that evening, when Sesame was alone in her room, she sat on her bed remembering some of the amazing things that had happened.

"The octopus looked SO scary," she told her teddy, Alfie. "At first I thought he was going to eat me. But he was great. I'm glad he gave those horrid pixies a hard time."

She opened her jewellery box; Queen Charm's silver bracelet and nine magical charms lay there. Sesame fished the mermaid purse from her pocket and took out the happy, playful dolphin charm.

"Look, Alfie," she whispered. "Isn't it lovely? Just like the real ones I saw today! Now there are only three more charms to find," she told him, as carefully she placed the dolphin in the box with the others.

68

Sesame was so pleased to have found the dolphin charm that she almost forgot what Selena had said about the purse. She remembered now: 'It contains something precious.'

She gave the purse a little shake and . . . out fell the photo of Poppy.

"Oh!" gasped Sesame, staring at the tiny image of her mother smiling back at her.

Tears trickled down her cheeks as she thought of her favourite necklace and how the pixies had taken it. Even worse, the wicked magician, Zorgan, might be holding it right now. She shuddered.

And then something dawned on her. Staring at Poppy, Sesame realised the *most* precious thing about her locket was what it contained. She treasured the little picture of her mum, and it was safe and sound. As for her dad . . . he was here, for real! Besides, she had loads more photos of him. Sesame wiped her tears. She placed the picture of Poppy inside the jewellery box with the charms — precious things together — and closed the lid. Things didn't seem so bad, after all.

Ten

Three magic candles remain burning for their charms yet to be found – the silver crescent moon, the cloverleaf and the key. A tell-tale wisp of smoke curls from the candle that bears the dolphin's name, and the Silversmith claps her hands with delight. She knows it safe with Sesame, in the Outworld.

Seated at her dressing table, she brushes her fine, silvery hair and thinks about the day she knows will soon come, when all the charms are found, and the magical bracelet will be returned to Queen Charm.

"Three more charms to find and Sesame will have completed her quest," she says. "Nothing, no *nothing* must stand in her way . . ."

As she speaks, the red sun rises and a ray of fiery sunshine strikes the mirror glass. For a split-second she is dazzled by the light; she rubs her eyes and looks again and now she sees the terrifying vision of Zorgan! The magician is scowling and from a finger he dangles a locket. It belongs to Sesame, of course, and the locket is open. The Silversmith peers more closely. The place where Poppy's picture should be is quite empty!

"Ah," she sighs, as the vision fades. "The Moon Spirits have worked their magic. All is not lost!"

But she knows her Seeker will be tested – it will take all Sesame's courage and strength to defeat Zorgan's tricks and treachery . . . but that is another story, it must be told another day!

Acknowledgments

I owe a debt of gratitude to all those who have worked behind the scenes at Orion Children's Books and beyond to bring the *Charmseekers* books and their thirteen delightful charms to you. Since it would take more space than this edition allows to mention individuals by name, suffice it to say that I'm hugely grateful to my publishers and everyone involved with the publication of this series. In particular, my special thanks go to: my publisher, Fiona Kennedy, for her faith in believing I could write way beyond my own expectations. Her creative, tactful and skilful editing kept Sesame Brown on the right track and helped me to write a better story; my agent, Rosemary Sandberg; Jenny Glencross and Jane Hughes (Editorial); Alex Nicholas and Helen Speedy (Rights) Loulou Clark and Helen Ewing (Design); Clare Hennessy (Production); Jessica Killingley and Jo Dawson (Marketing); Pandora White (Orion Audio Books); Imogen Adams (Website designer – www.hammerinheels.com); Neil Pymer, the *real* Spinner Shindigs, for kind permission to use his name; and last, but by no means least, a million thanks go to my husband Tom for his inexhaustible patience, critical appraisal and support along the way.

Georgie Adams